D1244753

MIRACLE AT EGG ROCK

MIRACLE AT EGG ROCK
A Puffin's Story

By Doris Gove

Illustrated by Bonnie Bishop

Copyright 1985 by Doris Gove
ISBN 0-89272-205-3
Library of Congress Catalog Card No. 85-07050

Designed by Bonnie Bishop
Composition by Roxmont Graphics
Printed at Capital City Press, Inc., Montpelier, Vt.

5   4   3   2   1

Down East Books, Camden, Maine 04843

For Laura Grace

Acknowledgments

*I would like to thank Dr. Stephen Kress
for commenting on technical details of this story
and for making many helpful suggestions.
Thanks also to Jeff Mellor,
who reread every small change that was made.*

What More Could a Tiny Puffin Want?

A flash of silver at the entrance of the tunnel caught her eye: fish — fresh, smooth, slippery fish. She was just barely awake, but she walked clumsily toward the entrance and ate all three of them headfirst. One of them tasted funny, but she swallowed it down just like the other two. She was hungry.

"Very good!" said a low voice from outside the tunnel. "Three smelt and a vitamin pill for this one."

"OK. We'll try four fish tomorrow. This one's band number will be 785-Q7582. Let's just call her Q7."

Q7 was a tiny puffin, just twelve days old. She was a little smaller than a tennis ball and covered with coal black, fuzzy down feathers. Her black webbed feet with their three long toes looked as if they were too big for her body.

When she was only a few days old, two National Audubon Society scientists had brought her to Egg Rock, a small, treeless, windy island near the coast of

Maine. They put her in a tunnel just like one that puffin parents would make for a nest. Some little roots and grass stems stuck out from the walls of the tunnel, and a screen covered the entrance. Q7 pulled pieces off the roots and grass to make a small nest where she could curl up.

Many years ago, there were lots of puffins on Egg Rock. Other ocean birds, such as Arctic terns, petrels, and laughing gulls, used to live there too. They raised their families on the island, and the ones that grew up there always came back when it was time for them to lay eggs. But about a hundred years ago, people started coming to Egg Rock. They stole the eggs and shot the birds until there wasn't even one puffin left.

Now laws protect the wildlife on the island, and the scientists are hoping that the puffins and the other birds will come back. Some birds, like terns, will be able to see that the island is safe again, and they will come back to nest there. But other birds, like puffins, will not nest in a new place. They will only nest on the same islands where they grew up.

The scientists don't know if the birds actually have to be hatched on the island to feel that it is their home, or if they just have to spend some of their growing-up time there. Q7, even though she didn't volunteer for the job, was part of an experiment to find out if there is a way to bring puffins back to live on Egg Rock.

Many puffins still live on islands in Canada, so the scientists have brought some young ones like Q7 from there and raised them on Egg Rock. They dug tunnels, caught fish to feed to the puffin chicks, kept seagulls away, and wrote lots of numbers in notebooks. What more could a tiny puffin want?

Q7 was too young to remember her mother and father, and the scientists who adopted her took good care of her. The tunnel was warm and dry, the fish were good, and she got to sleep as much as she needed. She was safe from hungry seagulls, which sometimes eat puffin chicks. She did have a problem with ticks — some had crawled up onto the skin around her eyes. She tried to scratch them off, but when she lifted one big foot to scratch, she fell over sideways. Rubbing her head against the dirt didn't help either.

One day Q7 heard someone coming and wobbled out to the entrance to get her fish. But instead, the tunnel suddenly got very dark. A huge hand reached in and strong, heavy fingers grabbed her. She wiggled free and ran as far back as she could. But the hand kept coming, and the fingers pulled her away from the back wall of the tunnel. She poked around for a soft place and bit as hard as she could.

"Ouch! Q7 is a strong one," said the same voice that counted out her fish each day. Q7 suddenly found herself lying on her back out in sunlight so hard and bright that her eyes hurt even though they were squeezed closed. She kicked her feet and felt like she was swinging in the air.

"She weighs 130.4 grams — not bad for two weeks old. It looks like we're feeding her the right kind of fish. First we'll get these ticks off her eyes, and then let's see how long her wings are."

Q7 squeezed her eyes even tighter as she felt something hard and cold against her eyelids. It did feel good to get rid of those itchy ticks, though. She tried to bite the big fingers again as her wings were pulled out straight to be measured. She was feeling awfully sick.

Then the big hand set her down gently at the entrance to the tunnel. She ran back into the darkness and collapsed onto her little nest. Covering her head with her wing, she went to sleep. She dreamed that big fingers came after her, and she gave one of them a good, hard bite.

Every day the fingers brought more fish — bigger, tastier ones than before. One always tasted a bit funny, but Q7 tossed them into the air and gulped them down too fast to care. The tunnel seemed to get smaller as she stretched, hopped, and flapped her wings against the walls and ceiling. She peeked out through the screen and saw long, wavy grass dancing in the wind. The light seemed warmer and not so scary. It didn't hurt her eyes any more.

Her feathers grew, and she spent hours smoothing them and covering them with oil from a little bump on her tail that was her oil gland. Soon her wing feathers were longer than her wings. She would rub her head back and forth on the oil gland until her head feathers and beak were shiny and looked wet. Then she rubbed her head along her back and pulled each long wing feather through her beak. When the feather snapped back into its place, it was smooth and looked as if it had been polished.

Her legs got stronger, too. She could stand on one foot and scratch the ticks away from her eyes with the other. But her feet still seemed to be too big.

She often walked out to the entrance of her tunnel and leaned against the screen that covered it, looking out or stretching up on her toes to look up. Silhouettes of flying birds floated overhead, and she could hear birds calling to each other. But if she heard any noise near the tunnel, she ran back to her dark, safe nest and waited, absolutely still, until the noise was gone. Sometimes she scratched at the dirt to make the tunnel longer, and then she felt even safer.

One afternoon she heard voices and a lot of footsteps. She ran as far back as she could and crouched, facing toward the bright tunnel entrance. The tunnel got completely dark as an arm and fingers reached in. Q7 pecked at the fingers and dug her feet into the dirt, but she wasn't strong enough to fight the big fingers. One of the scientists pulled her out into the light.

"It's your turn now, Q7," said the voice. "Everyone gets bird bands today. But after that, we won't bother you again."

10

The scientists quickly weighed her and measured her wings and wing feathers. She opened her eyes a little and twisted her head around, looking for her tunnel entrance. She suddenly noticed that there were lots of entrances just like hers. If she could jump and run, how would she find the right tunnel?

But she forgot about that problem when one of the scientists pulled her leg out straight and closed a pair of hard metal pliers around it. She squeezed her eyes tight, tried to scratch, bite, and kick, and then felt the cold pliers on the other leg. What were they doing to her legs?

"That's it, Q7! You're ready to go. Whatever you do, don't forget Egg Rock. We want you to come back."

The big hand set her down at the right tunnel entrance, waited until she got her balance, and then let her go. She ran back into the darkness and her little nest of roots and grass.

Her legs were fine except for a metal band around one leg that said:

ADVISE BIRD BAND
Washington DC
785-Q7582

On the other leg was a red and yellow plastic band that just had "95" on it. She pushed them, pulled them, scratched at them and pecked them until she was sore all over. They just wouldn't come off. Her feet were too big.

After dark that night, everything was very quiet. Q7 walked out to the tunnel entrance. The screen was gone, and she stuck her head out into the crisp, clear air. She stretched her neck so that she could see more, but kept her feet firmly inside the tunnel. Turning her head sideways to look up, she saw patterns of stars that looked like pictures.

Suddenly she noticed something move near the tunnel entrance next to hers. She jerked back into her tunnel, but then slowly and silently stuck her head out just

12

far enough to see around the edge. She found herself looking right into the face of another puffin chick! Its eyes shone in the starlight, and as they stared at each other, they both walked a little way out of their tunnels. Q7 saw that the other puffin had a band on each leg too. She gently touched its beak with hers, and then looked along the line of entrances. Five or six other young puffins stood in the darkness, turning their heads to look in all directions and stretching their wings.

Leaving Home

One late afternoon the fingers dropped more fish than they had ever brought before. This time, the fish were left outside the tunnel instead of inside. Q7 was as hungry as usual, and as soon as it was quiet again after the scientists left, she hurried outside into the light without even thinking. She gobbled up all the fish and stood blinking in the warm sunshine. The orange sun was disappearing into a low cloud bank.

It felt wonderful. Warm, wet wind pushed against her from all sides, playing a game of lifting a few feathers, brushing against her skin underneath them, and then pushing them flat again. She kept turning her head to see, but then the wind would be somewhere else. She stretched her neck and wings and spread her wing feathers out like a huge, black fan. She felt three times bigger than before. There were colors everywhere — blue sky, pink and orange sky, waving green grass, flowers. And from far away came a thundering, pounding noise, but somehow it wasn't scary. It was just like a deeper wind, and she felt that she would like to go find it. The sun sank some more and made the rocks and grass look orange.

14

Q7 started walking down the little hill in front of her tunnel. She bounced from side to side with each step, and her head bounced in a different rhythm than her body. She kept turning her head to look forward, first with one eye and then with the other. She twisted her neck so that one eye looked straight up into the sky, which seemed to have no end. At the same time the other eye saw a rock right under her feet, but too late. Q7 tripped and flopped sideways into the long grass. There must be a better way to get around, she thought.

The wind and the grass swirled in circles around her as she rested. She turned her head from side to side and saw new things in every direction.

She stood and faced the wind, spreading her wings to keep her balance. There was another big rock in front of her, but she couldn't see any grass beyond it. As she crawled up onto the rock, a feeling of lightness and happiness came over her. Suddenly she knew that if she flapped her wings, something wonderful would happen.

And it did. The wind helped by sending a warm gust under her wings, and her wing feathers pushed back at the wind until they pulled her whole body upright, and she stood on the tips of her toes. Then she rose into the air, flapping as hard as she could, as the wind boosted her up and whispered encouragement in her ears.

Suddenly she saw the ocean. It was spread out underneath her and looked as endless as the sky, but with a more brilliant blue. The waves made deep, dark valleys and white, lace-topped hills. Greenish-white foam crashed against Egg Rock, making a hollow roar, then a long sigh, then a roar again. Splashes of foam sprang into the air and rode on the wind.

Q7 flapped as hard as she could, but from time to time she just had to rest. She would slow down a bit and start to drift down toward the water. Then she would flap faster to go up again. She turned her head with quick little jerks to look down and up, forward with one eye and back with the other.

If she had looked back to the grassy part of the island, she would have seen hands and fingers waving to say good-bye as the sky got dark.

Finally her wings were too tired, and she drifted down to a soft, rolling wave. With a big splash and a belly-flop, she got water in her eyes and all over her wings and back. Her feet had never felt anything so cold. At first, she paddled quickly from one wave top to the next, but then she found that if she pulled her feet up into her belly feathers, they felt warmer. She reached back to the oil gland near her tail and squeezed some oil onto her beak and rubbed some into her head feathers. Then she cleaned and oiled all her feathers, and the cold ocean water couldn't seep through them toward her skin. She pulled her wings tight around her, tucked her head under one wing, and went to sleep.

The waves rocked and splashed her, and the wind tried to tease her by lifting her feathers. But flying was hard work, and Q7 bobbed up and down and didn't wake up until morning. A few stars twinkled in a dark blue sky, and mountains of water rose and fell as she slept.

In the east, the sky became clear and pink, and soon the huge orange sun lifted out of the water. Q7 felt her back feathers starting to get warm. She popped her head out from under her wing and moved it around in little jerks so that she could see in every direction. The silhouette of a seabird floated overhead, and Q7 turned her head sideways to watch it flying. Did I really do *that?* she wondered.

A Flash of Silver

Paddling rapidly, she leaped out of the water and flapped, splashing water off her wings and body. Her feet kept paddling, and it looked as if she were running across the top of the water. She flapped harder and harder and rose up just barely enough to get over the top of the next wave. But she was flying again — she could still do it. From the air she could see only the ocean. When she looked back toward Egg Rock, all she could see was fog. The sea was quiet. There were no rocks here for the water to crash against, and the tops of the waves just whispered in the wind. The pointed top of one big wave folded over on itself, and the noise and foam ran from one end of the wave to the other. Q7 watched as the greenish bubbles sank back into the wave.

A flash of silver sparkled just above the surface of the water. It was a tiny fish jumping, and Q7 suddenly realized that she was hungrier than she had ever been before. She flew down to the foamy white spot where the fish had been and slid

17

headfirst right into the water. This time, the water didn't get in her eyes because she closed her special underwater eyelids. She could see through these eyelids. They were like windows that she could pull sideways across her eyes to protect them when she swam underwater.

She saw lots of fish down there, but they were swimming very fast. Q7 flew through the water, using quick, strong strokes of her wings and pushing the water backward with her big webbed feet. There was a little fish right in front of her, swimming as fast as it could. Just as Q7 snapped her beak, the fish flipped its tail and dived. Q7 could feel it brush along her belly, but she couldn't turn fast enough to chase it. She looked around for another fish, but by the time she was close enough to any of them, she needed to come up for air.

She looked up and down, forward and back, and pretty soon she saw another fish jump. She paddled to the white spot where the fish had been and dived again. This time there were even more fish — so many that it seemed she could just open her mouth wide and she would bump into one. But each time she got close to some, they shot off in all directions, and then she was out of air again.

Q7 took a big gulp of air and then dived deeper than she had before. She saw one fish that seemed to be a little slower than the rest, and she turned both eyes forward so they focused on the fish like binoculars. The fish started down, and Q7 chased it faster and faster. Just as it flipped its tail to turn, her sharp beak closed over its tail fin. She popped up to the surface like a cork, tossed the fish up in the air, and swallowed it headfirst. It wiggled all the way down her throat.

After all that work, she felt even hungrier than before, and she spent the rest of the day chasing fish deep underwater. Most of them got away, but by the end of the day she had caught and eaten twelve fish, and she was more tired than hungry. So she tucked her head under her wing and went to sleep — not with a full stomach, but at least with something.

Each day, Q7 caught more of the fish that she chased. She learned how to pick out the slowest ones, and she learned all their tricks for escaping. She could tell if they were going to flip up or dive down, and her beak would move with them and then snap them up. For weeks, she stayed out of sight of land, all by herself except for a passing bird or ship once in a while. She caught short, fat fish and long, skinny fish, silver ones, black ones, fast ones, and slow ones. Every one of them was absolutely delicious. If there weren't any fish around, she would catch a little squid or a shrimp, but they weren't quite so good.

She got fatter, and her feathers became smoother. The little bits of baby down that used to stick out from the feathers on her head disappeared.

Sometimes she would fly up to look around and then splash down again; other times she would just paddle in one long, straight line for hours until she was too tired to move. With her head tucked under her wing and her feet wrapped in her belly feathers, she rocked to sleep each night.

The Whales and the Tourists

The weather was getting colder, and the wind seemed stronger and noisier than before. On some days, Q7 would fly closer to land, where she saw seagulls, guillemots, cormorants, and other birds. The seagulls knew everything, it seemed, and they never stopped telling everybody about it. Q7 was afraid of the gulls — they were big and fast, and their long hooked beaks opened very wide when they screamed. But Q7 could paddle pretty fast herself by now, and she could always dive deep or fly up and leave if she got scared. So one day she let herself float closer to one group of gulls to see what all the noise was about.

"Whale! Whale! Whale!" cried several seagulls all at once, as an explosion of water spouted up very near where Q7 was resting on the water. A monstrous rubbery black and white body, bigger than a boat, bobbed up beside her. Spray spouted again from its head. Q7 wondered whether she ought to fly away from this huge thing. But the seagulls didn't fly off the way they would if this creature were

20

dangerous. Instead, they floated in the air and turned their heads from side to side so they wouldn't miss anything.

Q7 paddled closer and inspected the whale with one eye and then with the other. Even if she stretched out her head and neck as far as possible, she couldn't see the ends of its body. Once she thought she saw a little black eye on the side of its huge head, but a wave splashed up and all she could see was the shiny smooth body. Then the whale made a gigantic splash with its wide, flat tail and disappeared, leaving a rolling mound of bubbles and making a wave that tossed Q7 sideways on the water. She had to stick out her wings to keep her balance, and even then the wave rose over her and knocked her completely under water.

"Tourists! Tourists! Tourists!" called some seagulls from the air.

A small, lopsided boat with twenty heads leaning over one side was moving toward the whale's bubbles. The people were waving and pointing, and a loud voice came from the top of the boat.

"And now, off to your right, ladies and gentlemen, a fin whale has just spouted. You can tell it apart from the humpback whale that we saw earlier because the plume is higher and thinner. And that wave and mound of smooth water where the whale was — it's like the whale's footprint. You can always identify the kind of whale by the wave that it leaves. Oh, look! That bird on the edge of the wave, just coming up from a dunking — that's an Atlantic puffin. Look at its big beak. This one is a young bird and doesn't have the bright-colored bill that most people expect to see on puffins. . . . And there it goes."

Q7 flapped hard to lift her body above the waves and headed out to sea. She didn't like twenty pairs of binoculars, hands, and fingers all pointing at her. It was time to leave.

"That puffin is banded," boomed the voice behind her. "It may be from the Egg Rock Project."

Two more fin whales spouted to the left of the boat, which tipped and tossed to the other side as all the people ran to the opposite rail. Q7 couldn't see the heads any more.

"Our porpoises are back, too." The voice from the boat was fading. Q7 looked back toward the boat and saw three shiny porpoises leap in front of the waves. Their bodies were tightly curved as they seemed to bounce out of the water. Then the boat faded from her view as she kept flying.

"Food! Food! Good food!" screamed several seagulls all at once. Q7 peered down at the circle of gulls around a red fishing boat. They wheeled and dived to catch some fish heads and half a hamburger wrapped in white paper. Seagulls will eat anything, thought Q7, who considered food to be no good to eat if it wasn't wiggling. She flew until she got so far out that she couldn't see any more small boats or seagulls, then drifted down to the water. Waves rocked her, and she tucked her head under her wing for a nap.

When she woke up, she looked around and noticed two whales spouting water, and she watched them raise their tails and dive. Then she dived herself to catch some fish. But just as she was about to grab a herring, she heard a piercing whistle, then some loud squeaks, a roar, and then some more whistling and a noise like the motor of a fishing boat. She popped up to the surface and looked everywhere. There were no boats, no gulls, nothing except open water in all directions.

She dived again. The funny noises seemed to be far away, so she swam toward them. There were squeaks and moans, grumbles and growls. A squeal started and got louder and higher until Q7's ears hurt. Then there was a rumble, like the sound of water rushing between two big rocks.

The sounds came from two different directions, and they seemed to be

23

answering each other. Q7 got closer to one of them and peered through the green water. Suddenly she saw the shadowy outline of the humpback whale moving slowly along, waving its tail up and down. It was singing! It made a long, drawn-out squeal, and then an answering squeal came from somewhere far away.

Q7 was so surprised that she almost forgot she needed air, but then she came up and floated on the waves for a while. Every few minutes, she dived down again to listen to the whale songs.

A Funny Name for a Puffin

The wind was always with her. Some days it felt nice, and she would stretch her head and neck out and open her wings so that the wind would ruffle her feathers. Then she would smooth them all down again with a fresh coat of oil. But other days, the wind whistled and roared, sometimes so hard that Q7 was afraid to fly in it. She would be tossed and splashed by waves moving in every direction, and if it got too rough, she would dive and stay under water as long as she could.

Sometimes the wind would rush around in circles for hours, slamming hard raindrops onto her back. She would have to oil her feathers several times a day to keep her skin warm and dry. One storm lasted for a week. The ocean water was hard and gray, and she couldn't catch any fish. The wind was too rough to fly in, and she got very cold and hungry as she bounced around on the tall waves.

Then the water turned blue and sparkling again. The wind played games and the fish jumped, flashing their silvery bodies.

One gray day, Q7 popped her head out from under her wing and looked up and down, forward and back. She was close enough to land to see a few seagulls, but they seemed strangely quiet, sitting on the water and turning their heads from side to side. Even the waves hitting the rocks seemed muffled. One seagull flew in to join the group.

"Sno-ow! Sno-ow! Cold sno-ow!" it called in a low voice just before it landed and pulled its head and neck back between hunched shoulders. The other gulls and Q7 fluffed up their feathers and drew their bodies deeper into them. Q7 kept her feet tight up against her belly to be warmer. She couldn't paddle that way, and just drifted up one side of a wave and then down the other. White snowflakes swirled around her. They disappeared into the water, but piled up on her back. Soon the air was solid white, and she couldn't see the land or the gulls any more. But when the sound of the waves told her she was getting too close to the rocks, she put her head down and paddled in a straight line out to sea.

The snow fell for three days. When the sky finally cleared, Q7 cleaned her feathers and looked around for signs of fish. In the distance she could see a small island. The shape of the island looked familiar, but the color was different — it was completely white except for a dark green spruce tree on the highest point. When the wind blew, ribbons of white snow came off the branches of the spruce tree.

For the rest of the winter, Q7 tried to stay away from the worst blizzards by flying miles and miles from the black clouds that dropped white snow. Some days there was no escape, though, so at those times she tucked her head under her wing, pulled her feet up into her belly feathers, and drifted on the waves. When she popped her head out to look in all directions, sometimes she saw only black walls of hard, cold water so tall that they seemed about to close over her. But in the next second she would be at the top of a wave looking out across other peaks and valleys. She fluffed and oiled her feathers whenever the winter storms gave her a chance, and she caught fish when the pale sun managed to light the water from black to gray.

She met other puffins during these gray days. When she saw one on the water, she would drop down and touch its beak with hers. They would sit quietly for a few moments, and then each one would fly off to be alone on the great ocean again. But during these short visits, she learned many things that most puffins learn from their parents in the nest tunnel.

"We are the three-toed birds," one puffin told her. "Puffins, murres, and auks. You'll need your long toenails when you grow up and dig a nest tunnel. Those seagulls — they have four toes. And they eat garbage."

"Watch out for the biggest gulls — the ones with black backs and the red spots on their beaks," said another puffin. "They can be dangerous."

One day she was swimming under water after sand eels, one of her favorite fish. She snapped up two little eels out of a large school, and started up to the surface to swallow them. Above her in the water she saw a pair of feet paddling, and then she saw a puffin that she hadn't met before. He was a first-year puffin like her; she could tell because his beak had just one ridge on it like hers.

"What's your name?" she asked, as soon as the eels stopped wiggling in her throat.

"Little Brother. What's yours?"

"Q7."

"That's a funny name for a puffin. What island are you from?"

"Egg Rock."

Little Brother looked at her with one eye and then with the other. "I've heard of Egg Rock," he said. "But I thought that puffins didn't nest there any more. The eggeaters killed them all."

"Egg — eaters?"

"Yes. Monsters with arms and fingers instead of wings. They can reach into tunnels and pull out eggs or babies. Or sometimes they catch puffins with ropes and twist their necks. My mother told me stories about them. We can't nest near the eggeaters any more."

Little Brother told Q7 the story of the Great Auk, another three-toed bird. It was a wonderful swimmer, but it couldn't fly, and it nested on just a few islands. Long ago, eggeaters came in small boats that were pointed on both ends and about as big as porpoises. They would steal a few eggs and take two or three birds — no more during the summer than the black-backed gulls took.

But later, other eggeaters came in huge boats that were bigger than whales. They had nets, guns, and long poles with hooks on the ends. They killed auks and puffins and piled them in the boats along with baskets of eggs. A few days later, they would come back for more. Since the Great Auks couldn't fly, the eggeaters soon caught them all.

"Now we have to nest far away from eggeaters," said Little Brother.

Q7 told him about the hands and fingers that had fed her fish on Egg Rock and how they put the bands on her legs.

"They sound like eggeaters too," said Little Brother. "But maybe they are a different kind."

Q7 had never talked to anyone for so long before. Off to one side, a herring flashed underwater and she dived after it. When she came up several yards away with the fish in her mouth, she glanced back. Little Brother was still there, but raising his wings, getting ready to take off.

"I'll see you when it gets warm," he called over the wind. "I've heard that puffins get together near the nesting islands on pretty days."

Little Brother flapped away. Q7 wondered if she'd see him again, but right then, there were more herrings and sand eels to catch.

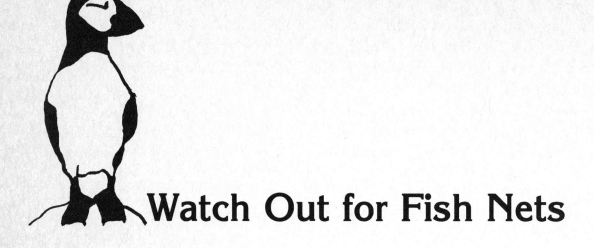

Watch Out for Fish Nets

It did start getting warmer. The sun looked orange in the mornings and evenings. The sky and the water turned blue again. Q7 could feel warmth creeping through her back feathers. She stretched her wings, neck, and feet out as far as she could, and carefully oiled and fixed her feathers.

Fish jumped in the sunlight and dashed through the water in big schools that suddenly changed direction as if all the fish were part of one body. Smelts, herrings, and sand eels were everywhere. Q7 learned to dive right underneath a school so she could look up and see the fish against the light. It was easier to catch them this way. She could catch two or three at a time and hold them against the top of her mouth until she came up to the surface to swallow them.

One day she was underneath an especially good school of fat smelts. Some of them were too big for her to swallow, so she only chased the little ones. She had one in her mouth and was swimming after another one, when suddenly the fish scattered in all directions and a great wave rushed through the water. Q7 forgot

30

about catching the second fish and dived down to escape. But after just a few strokes, she hit the hard, tight ropes of a fishing net. It was moving up through the water, and the fish trapped in the net were bumping into her and starting to pile up on top of each other.

Q7 needed air. She turned around and pushed up through the flopping fish. Just as she reached the surface and got one breath, another part of the net pulled her back under again, and she felt herself rolling and tumbling sideways and then upside down, completely buried in piles of frightened, jumping fish.

The net burst out of the water and swung through the air toward a fishing boat. Q7 stretched her head and neck through the slippery fish bodies and opened her beak wide. She lay on her side gasping for air. Fish, water, squid, and shrimp slid around her and through her feathers.

The net opened, and everything inside fell into a big wooden tray on the deck of the boat. Q7 felt sick. She just lay with her eyes closed, gasping for air. She heard crashes and thumps as the net hit the sides of the tray.

"Hey! What's that black thing? I thought this was a school of smelts," said a voice from above the tray. Q7 felt herself moving again as rough fingers pushed the fish off her and lifted her out.

"It looks like a puffin — or a rock bird, we used to call them," said another voice. "Just a young one — no fancy colors yet. Look! It's still alive, and it's trying to breathe."

"Well, let's get rid of it. These things eat our fish, don't they?"

"Oh, they just eat the little ones, like the ones we throw back anyway. In fact, sometimes they are good for the fish. They catch fish that are sick, and then the others don't get the disease. What's that on its legs?"

Q7 closed her mouth and opened one eye a little as the man pulled her legs out straight to read the numbers on her bands.

"'785-Q7582.' Let's write that down. 'Advise Bird Band, Washington, D.C.' I guess that means we can write and tell them we found this puffin. Maybe they'll tell us where it came from and why they banded it."

The man held her wings closed with one hand and started drying her feathers with a towel. He was gentle and only rubbed the feathers from front to back. Q7 tried to bite the fingers, but she couldn't twist her neck around, and anyway, she felt too exhausted to try very hard. Warmth from his hand moved through her feathers to her wet skin, and she began to feel a bit better. She opened her eyes and looked up and down, forward and back.

"It seems to be feeling better. I'll hold it until it's dry and then let it go." He wrapped her in a dry towel and held her with both hands.

After a few minutes, he set her feet on the rail of the boat. As soon as she curled her toes around and tried to stand up, he let go of her wings. She pushed off the rail as hard as she could and flapped away, trying to decide whether to dive into the water or to fly up.

"Stay away from fish nets!" shouted the man after her. Q7 was tired, so she dropped down to the water and dived, swimming underwater as far as she could in a straight line until she had to come up for air. Then she paddled for a while, until no land or boats or seagulls could be seen. She settled down to a bigger feather cleaning job than she had ever had before. Fish scales, slime, and bits of seaweed had to be pulled out from under her feathers, and when she reached her head back to her oil gland, she could feel sore muscles all over her body.

After that, Q7 fished more carefully. She watched for fishing boats and swam away whenever she saw one, and she also listened more to the seagulls, who often followed the boats, hoping to steal some of the fish. She spent her days flying and fishing, and as the weeks passed, her feathers began to get smoother and more white appeared on her belly and cheeks.

Oil Boat

Q7 began to notice changes in the older puffins she met on the warm, sunny days. Their big triangular beaks grew even larger, until they seemed too heavy for their round heads. The end of each beak looked like a bright red lobster claw, and in back of that, two thick yellow ridges made a shape like a crescent moon around a dark blue patch. At the corners of their mouths were orange folds of skin shaped like little flowers. Around the eyes of the adult puffins, patches of hard, dark skin with no feathers made the eyes look bigger against their white cheeks.

Whenever Q7 came near these other puffins, she stared and stared. They looked splendid, but they never talked to her. They would look at her with one eye and then the other, and then ignore her as they oiled their beautiful new feathers to make them even shinier.

These dressed-up puffins were easier to see on the water than plain gray and black puffins like Q7. When she flew near land, sometimes she'd see four or five of

34

them drifting together, looking at each other and occasionally touching each other's beaks. If she flew down to join them, they paid no attention to her. They only looked at each other, and they often opened their beaks wide and showed their orange tongues. Even their feet were different from hers. Once Q7 came up from a dive near two adults, and she noticed that their feet were bright red with shiny black toenails. When she popped up close to them, they turned away and paddled off, so she flew away to fish on her own.

One day Q7 was asleep with her head under her wing, and some seagull calls woke her up.

"Oil boat! Oil boat! Oil boat!"

She looked up and down, forward and back, and even poked her head under water, but didn't see anything unusual. She decided to clean a few feathers and then go back to sleep.

But when she started to pull her tail feathers through her beak, she tasted something terrible. She shook a sticky glob of something out of her beak. Some of her feathers broke when she tried to clean them. Then she noticed that all around her were more little black globs, and the water had a covering that looked gray on the waves but flashed rainbow colors where the water was smooth. Her tail feathers had dipped into the oil on one side, and a spot had splashed up onto her back feathers. She paddled away as fast as she could, but the oil seemed to follow her. On one side it was getting close to her wings. It was time to leave.

As she rose high above the waves, she followed the oil slick with her eyes. At the end of it was the largest boat she had ever seen — big enough for many whales to lie across its deck. The people on the boat were washing out the inside by pumping ocean water through it. Dirty water gushed from a pipe on the side of the boat, and the oil spread out like fingers from where it splashed into the ocean water.

When Q7 flew high enough that she could see both ends of the oil boat, she could also see people as small as ticks moving about on its deck.

Her back felt cold. The oil from the boat had removed the waterproofing from one place on her feathers, and cold water had seeped through to her skin. As she flew, it dried out some, but the feathers that had touched the oil were rough and stiff. She flapped harder to get warmer. The terrible taste was still in her mouth. After several miles, she landed and then felt a bit of cold water on her skin again. It took hours of scrubbing with her beak to get her feathers smooth. Then she made them waterproof again with her own clear, clean feather oil.

Hot summer weather came, and there were more fish than ever. In good weather, Q7 would go for long flights. Once she flew east for several days without seeing any land. Then she came to a place with many islands and strange birds that she had never seen before. Some of the fish tasted different, too.

By following the patterns of the stars she always knew how to get back home, and after every long trip, she would spend some time in sight of islands that she could recognize by their shapes. Later, during the fall and winter, she stayed near those familiar islands. By now, she knew exactly where the best fish could be caught. Her second winter was just as cold as the first one, but she was bigger and had thicker feathers now, and it seemed a little easier.

A Baby Has Hatched

In late spring and summer, Q7 found larger groups of puffins sitting in the water near the islands. As she flew down to join them, she saw adult puffins, with their bright beaks and feet, standing on high rocks or walking back and forth with bouncing steps on the grass in front of nest tunnels. These were the nesting areas, and she met other young puffins like herself on the water near the islands.

One day she noticed an adult puffin flying close to the water carrying six fish in its beak: five short, fat smelts and one long, skinny sand eel. The heads were hanging out one side of its beak and the tails wiggled up and down on the other side. Every puffin on the water turned its head sideways to watch as the puffin with fish landed on the rock, flapped its wings a few times, and then disappeared into a nest tunnel.

"A baby has hatched!" explained a puffin that Q7 had just met. "The first baby of the year. Now you're not the youngest any more."

Within a few days, there was a steady stream of mother and father puffins coming in with fish hanging out of their mouths. Sometimes a seagull would fly down and peck at one of them before it could duck into its nest tunnel. The puffin would drop all of its fish and run away from the sharp beak of the seagull, who would then walk around and gobble up the fish.

Q7 spent most of her time by herself fishing far from the sight of land. But every few days she would fly to one of the nesting areas and drift down to the water with other puffins. She would sit there bobbing up and down and turning her head in little jerks to see everything that was going on. She met Little Brother again at one nesting area with high cliffs and crashing waves.

"This is where I hatched," he said. "My mother and father have a new baby this year."

Spring moved into summer, with hot windy days, stormy days with thunder and lightning bursting out of black clouds, and foggy mornings when it was almost as hard to see as in last winter's snowstorms. Mother and father puffins fished in all kinds of weather, and they carried bigger and bigger loads of fish back to their babies in the tunnels. Q7 could see them fishing when she was far from any nesting area. Even when their beaks were so full of wriggling fish that it seemed they couldn't hold even one more, they would keep diving. Then finally, with water streaming off their heads and backs and the little dangling fish tails, they would flap hard to get just above the waves and take off in a straight line toward their island.

But suddenly it all stopped. Adult puffins rested in groups near the islands or flew in lazy, wandering flights. Their fine feathers looked worn and dirty, and the brilliant designs on their beaks peeled and fell off.

"But where are the babies?" Q7 asked a tired-looking puffin floating near her.

"Oh, they'll come out of the tunnels when they get hungry enough. From now on, they have to learn to catch their own fish."

A week later she did see some baby puffins on the water. Their heads were gray, with little tufts of baby down poking up from their feathers. They looked thin and clumsy, but they were catching fish.

Cold, windy weather returned, and Q7 remembered how to watch for dark clouds and to stay out of the worst storms. For weeks at a time, she didn't see any other birds, and she didn't fly much because the wind was so strong.

A Place for a Nest

But her third winter went by fast, and another nesting season started. Q7 now had a thick ridge on her own beak, and her beak was yellow and orange instead of plain black. From time to time she met Little Brother near an island, and they would fly together for a few days, looking for good fishing spots or dropping in on a nesting area together. Sometimes they tried to see who could catch the most fish in one mouthful without dropping one.

One day they were flying southeast after a long fishing trip. They passed the Matinicus Rock lighthouse and made a big half circle to keep from getting too close to a fishing boat. Q7 recognized Egg Rock in the distance and turned toward it. Little Brother followed behind, and they floated down to a quiet spot on the water where they would be protected from the wind. The island looked like a good puffin nesting place, but there were no birds flying out with empty beaks and back with full beaks. All they could see was bare rocks and grass waving in the wind.

But as they paddled along looking at the island, they saw three puffins standing very still beside a metal thing that flashed in the sunlight.

"Let's go up there and look around," said Q7.

"And land on rocks? I haven't touched a rock since the day I left my nest tunnel! And what about the eggeaters?"

"I haven't stood on a rock since then either. I don't see any eggeaters. Let's try it — those puffins up there aren't worried."

They flew up and came in toward a big rock. They spread their feet out wide for the landing, plopped down, and lost their balance. After a few clumsy steps, they stumbled down toward the grass, which was softer, but it got tangled around their feet. In front of them on a flat rock stood the three puffins. They still hadn't moved.

Q7 and Little Brother pushed through the grass toward the rock. As soon as they got to the edge of it, they found that they could use their long toenails on rough parts of the rock to keep their balance. Walking became a little easier. The three strange puffins were colored like adults, with yellow and orange beaks and red eyes. But they didn't turn away as adult puffins usually did. They didn't even turn their heads to watch out for danger. Little Brother came close to one of them and touched its beak with his. Nothing happened. He pecked at it a little harder, and then pecked it on the head. It was hard — not soft like feathers. Little Brother and Q7 pecked at the head at the same time, and the strange puffin stared past them without moving.

"These aren't real puffins," said Little Brother. "They feel like the pieces of wood that we see floating in the water."

But Q7 wasn't listening to him. She was looking into the metal thing that flashed in the sun, and she did see a puffin that moved. When she moved, it moved, and when she stared with one eye and then with the other, it did the same thing.

Then she saw Little Brother beside her and also beside the puffin that she was looking at.

"It's a reflection," she said. "It's like when the water is so smooth in the morning that you can see yourself in it."

Q7 and Little Brother looked at the reflection and at the three wooden puffins that just stared into space. Then they turned and scrambled down the rock, spreading their wings to keep from falling. At the base of the rock, Q7 scratched at some loose dirt with her long toenails.

"Here's a place where we could make a tunnel," said Q7. She poked her head under a rock into a little space.

"Here's another," said Little Brother. "I've heard that it's very hard to make a nest tunnel on my island because the old puffins own all the good land already. There's just no more room."

"It would be easy here — and look at this one."

Each of them found several good places, but they kept coming back to the one with loose dirt under a rock. It had a big patch of grass in front, and beyond that was a clear view of the ocean. They took turns pecking at the dirt and made a hole almost big enough to wriggle into.

"I know that there's good fishing here," said Q7.

"But do you think it's a safe place?" asked Little Brother.

"It was safe enough for me to grow up here. Besides, this just *feels* like the right place to dig a tunnel and raise chicks."

By now, their feet and leg muscles were very tired. They rested for a few minutes, looking in every direction. Then they walked back past the wooden puffins and up to the highest rock. They cleaned the dirt off their feathers and jumped off, drifting down to the water. They paddled for a while and then put their heads under their wings for a nap.

If they had walked across the island, they would have seen a long row of cozy nesting tunnels with screens over the fronts. Downhill from the tunnels was a small brown cabin with windows on each side. The two scientists who took care of the baby puffins stayed in the cabin, and they were both working that day. One was scooping fish out of a pail and stuffing a tiny vitamin pill into each fish mouth. The other one had a pair of binoculars hanging around her neck, and she was carefully writing up the report for the day in the best scientific language possible:

"Great news! Hurrah! What a day!" read the report in an official red notebook. "Two puffins were seen on the eastern part of Egg Rock at 1512 hours. One was banded — red-yellow on left leg. According to our records, this is 785-Q7582, female, hatched four summers ago and transplanted here to Egg Rock. This is the same puffin that was caught in a fishnet and released by two fishermen east of Matinicus Rock. The other one was unbanded, about the same age, and had a slightly larger head, so may be a male. The two puffins stayed on the island for 37 minutes and 45 seconds. They first examined our decoys and mirror, but lost interest in them after pecking at them a few times. Then they poked their heads under rocks and into hollow places, touched each other on the beak 21 times, and stayed close together, almost as if they were discussing something very important. These behaviors are identical to prenesting behaviors seen in the Canadian puffin nesting areas. So we can hope that this puffin and her mate will return next spring to nest here.

"785-Q7582 is the first puffin of the Egg Rock Project to return to Egg Rock."

Epilogue

The miracle really happened — puffins came back to Egg Rock. For nearly a hundred years after people killed the last puffins on the islands close to the coast of Maine, no puffin chicks grew up in tunnels there, and no parents landed on the rocks with fish dangling from their beaks. A few puffins nested on Matinicus Rock, which was farther from the coast, but the nearest large puffin colonies were about nine hundred miles away, in Canada.

The project to bring puffins back to the Maine Islands was started by Dr. Stephen Kress of the National Audubon Society. First, Dr. Kress had to show Canadian wildlife scientists that he and his volunteers could raise puffin chicks successfully. Then the Canadian government let him collect one hundred baby puffins each year.

Some colonies in Canada still have thousands of puffins, so taking a few babies doesn't hurt the colony, even though puffins like Q7's parents probably feel bad when they lose their chick. Some colonies aren't as safe as they used to be because rats and seagulls have invaded them. Since female puffins only lay one egg a year, puffin colonies must be well protected for the species to survive. The more places there are that puffins can live, the safer they are from extinction. Egg Rock and other Maine islands are good, safe homes for sea birds now because the National Audubon Society and the U.S. Wildlife Service protect them. What happened to the puffins a century ago cannot happen again.

By 1981, 728 young adopted puffins on Egg Rock had eaten fish with vitamin pills in their mouths, had crawled out of nest tunnels, and had learned to fly, swim, and catch fish. Like Q7, all of these puffins spent at least three or four years alone at sea. The scientists kept working even though all their adopted puffins seemed to have disappeared. They wondered if the puffins would find enough fish, or if they might get caught and drowned in fish nets or oil spills, or if hungry black-backed gulls might swoop down and eat them. Some of the young puffins weren't as lucky as Q7 and Little Brother, but by 1981 the scientists had seen more than 100 of their 728 puffins back near Egg Rock, and they hope that more will fly in from the ocean every year. The scientists can recognize the puffins by their leg bands, and they keep careful records of where and when each bird is seen.

In 1981, two puffin babies hatched on Egg Rock. Their parents, who had been raised by the scientists, raised their own babies well (though without vitamin pills). Just before the new chicks were big enough to come out of the tunnels, the scientists put leg bands (-A- and -B-) on them. Two years later, Puffin B (another funny name for a puffin) was seen by scientists on Matinicus Rock. In 1984, he visited Egg Rock. And every year since 1981, puffins have nested successfully at Egg Rock.

Dr. Kress is now raising puffins on nearby Seal Island. So while puffins like Q7 raise their own chicks on Egg Rock, scientists will raise others a few miles away. In five years, there should be hundreds of healthy puffins who grew up on the Maine coast and think of it as their home. Then, it is hoped, the puffin colonies will be large enough to get along with no extra help from the scientists.

Now Maine puffins can again fish, fly, swim, have adventures, and listen to whale songs. And when they meet each other in the open ocean or at the nesting areas, they can tell stories about the places where puffins can live now and about the different kind of eggeaters who now protect them.

About the Author

Doris Gove teaches Biology at the University of Tennessee, and has in the past worked at a state park, a city nature center, and a biology research station as an environmental educator. She has also taught with the Peace Corps in Africa. In addition to her scholarly publications she writes freelance natural history articles. This is her first book.